A Note from

Robert Munsch

A long, long, LONG time ago when I was in first grade, my class had 60 kids in it!

The teacher didn't read any books and neither did the kids. It was not fun.

Well, here is a book that is fun to read for both you and your grown-ups.

READERS RULE!

High-Frequency Words

Practice reading these high-frequency words in the story:

all   down   new   over

Meet the Characters

Get to know the characters from the story by looking at the pictures and names below:

Jule Ann

Mommy

Mud Puddle

Character Spotlight: The Mud Puddle

Think about the mud puddle as a character in the story. Why do you think the mud puddle keeps trying to land on Jule Ann? If you had to draw a face for the mud puddle, what kind of expression would it have (e.g., happy, silly, sad, angry)?

Compound Words:

Some words have two words put together to make one word. These are called compound words. In this story, you can see the word "outside" which is made up of the words, "out" and "side." Take a look at the words below and turn them into compound words:

in	side
mail	box
snow	ball
ice	cream
star	fish

Can you think of any other compound words?

Phonics

There is an **M** sound at the beginning of the word **mud**.

Can you make an **M** sound?

Pay close attention to the shape of your mouth as you make the sound. It might be helpful to make this sound while you look in a mirror to see the shape your mouth makes.

Try these different activities to help practice the letter **M** sound.

1. Take a close look around you and try to find three objects that start with the same sound.

2. Think of three other words that also start with the same sound. As an extra challenge, can you think of any words that end with an **M** sound?

3. A simple word that has the **M** sound at the beginning is the word **mud**. As you read this word, pay attention to the two other letter sounds in the word.

4. When two words rhyme, they have the same sounds at the end of the word. Take a look at the pictures below and point to any of the words that rhyme with **mud**.

blood   **bud**   **moose**

5. While you read, look out for other **M** sounds at the beginning of a word throughout the story. You can see the sound easily because it will be written in a different color.

MUD PUDDLE

Story by Robert Munsch
Art by Dušan Petričić

annick
press
toronto • berkeley

Jule Ann put on her clean new
shirt and her clean new pants.

Then she went outside and sat
under a tree.

Up in the tree was a mud puddle.

It jumped right onto Jule Ann's head.

She was muddy all over.

"Mommy, Mommy! A mud puddle jumped on me," yelled Jule Ann.

Her mother dropped Jule Ann into the tub.

She washed out her ears and her eyes.

She even washed out her mouth.

Jule Ann put on a clean new shirt and clean new pants.

She went outside and sat down in her sandbox.

On top of the house was a mud puddle.

It jumped right onto Jule Ann's head.

She was muddy all over.

"Mommy, Mommy! A mud puddle jumped on me," yelled Jule Ann.

Her mother dropped Jule Ann into the tub.

She washed out her ears, her eyes, and her mouth.

She even washed out her nose.

Jule Ann had an idea.

She found a big yellow raincoat in the closet and put it on.

"Hey, Mud Puddle!" yelled Jule Ann.

Nothing happened.

Jule Ann took off her raincoat.

From behind the doghouse came the

mud puddle and jumped right onto

Jule Ann's head.

She was muddy all over.

"Mommy, Mommy! A mud puddle jumped on me," yelled Jule Ann.

Her mother dropped Jule Ann into the tub.

She washed out her ears, her eyes, her mouth, and her nose.

She even washed out her belly button.

Jule Ann put on a clean new shirt and clean new pants.

But she was afraid to go outside.

Then she had an idea.

She found a bar of smelly yellow soap.

Jule Ann ran outside and yelled,

"Hey, Mud Puddle!"

The mud puddle jumped over the

fence and ran right toward her.

Jule Ann threw the bar of soap

right in the mud puddle's middle.

"Awk, yecch, wackh!"

yelled the mud puddle.

The mud puddle ran across

the grass, jumped over the

fence, and never came back.

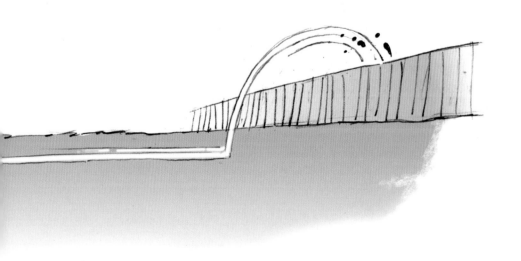

Getting Ready for Reading Tips

- Pick a time during the day when you are most excited to read. This could be when you wake up, after a meal, or right before bedtime.

- Create a special space in your home for reading with some blankets and pillows. The inside of a closet, under a table, or under a bed can make the perfect cozy spot.

- Before you start reading, do a quick look at all the pictures and suggest what the story might be about.

- Can you find the part of the story that repeats?

- Can you add actions like claps, stomps, or jumps to match what is being said to make the words come alive?

- Try to use silly voices for the different characters in the story. Think about changing the volume (e.g., loud, soft), the speed you use to say the words (e.g., fast, super slowly), and how you say the words (e.g., like an animal, like a superhero, like someone older or younger).

- What makes this story silly or funny?

- What part(s) of the story would never happen in real life?

Collect them all!

Adapted from the originals for beginner readers and packed with **Classic Munsch** fun!

Munsch Early Readers

Reading Level 3

50 BELOW ZERO

Story by **Robert Munsch**
Art by **Michael Martchenko**

Munsch Early Readers

Reading Level 3

I HAVE TO GO!

Story by **Robert Munsch**
Art by **Michael Martchenko**

Munsch Early Readers

Reading Level 3

MORTIMER

Story by **Robert Munsch**
Art by **Michael Martchenko**

Munsch Early Readers

Reading Level 3

PIGS

Story by **Robert Munsch**
Art by **Michael Martchenko**

Munsch Early Readers

Reading Level 3

The Paper Bag Princess

Story by **Robert Munsch**
Art by **Michael Martchenko**

All **Munsch Early Readers** are level 3, perfect for emergent readers ready for reading by themselves—because

READERS RULE!

Robert Munsch, author of such classics as *The Paper Bag Princess* and *Mortimer*, is one of North America's bestselling authors of children's books. His books have sold over 80 million copies worldwide. Born in Pennsylvania, he now lives in Ontario.

Dušan Petričić's brilliant illustrations have appeared around the world in newspapers, magazines, and award-winning picture books including *The Man With the Violin*, *Mattland*, and *My Toronto*. Dušan lives in Zemun, Serbia.

© 2022 Bob Munsch Enterprises Ltd. (text)
© 2022 Dušan Petričić (illustrations)

Original publication:
© 1979, 2012 Bob Munsch Enterprises Ltd. (text)
© 2012 Dušan Petričić (illustrations)

Designed by Leor Boshi

Thank you to Abby Smart, B.Ed., B.A. (Honors), for her work on the educational exercises and for her expert review.

Annick Press Ltd.

We acknowledge the support of the Canada Council for the Arts and the Ontario Arts Council, and the participation of the Government of Canada/la participation du gouvernement du Canada for our publishing activities.

ONTARIO ARTS COUNCIL
CONSEIL DES ARTS DE L'ONTARIO
an Ontario government agency
un organisme du gouvernement de l'Ontario

Library and Archives Canada Cataloguing in Publication

Title: Mud puddle / story by Robert Munsch ; art by Dušan Petričić.
Names: Munsch, Robert N., 1945- author. | Petričić, Dušan, illustrator.
Description: Series statement: Munsch early readers | Reading level 3: reading with help.
Identifiers: Canadiana (print) 20220170959 | Canadiana (ebook) 20220170967 | ISBN 9781773216584 (hardcover) | ISBN 9781773216485 (softcover) | ISBN 9781773216720 (HTML) | ISBN 9781773216843 (PDF)
Subjects: LCSH: Readers (Primary) | LCGFT: Readers (Publications)
Classification: LCC PE1119.2 .M8615 2022 | DDC j428.6/2—dc23

Published in the U.S.A. by Annick Press (U.S.) Ltd.
Distributed in Canada by University of Toronto Press.
Distributed in the U.S.A. by Publishers Group West.

Printed in China

annickpress.com
robertmunsch.com

Also available as an e-book. Please visit annickpress.com/ebooks for more details.